WITHDRAWN

No longer the property of the
Library.

Sale its the Library

D0983122

WITHDRAWN
No longer the property of the
Boston Public Library.
Sale of this material benefits the Library.

Charlie Cook's Favorite Book

SHIVER ME TIMBERS

FAIRY TALES
FROM A FORGOTTEN ISLAND

THE BEARO ANNUAL

JOUST JOKING!

REAL BIRDS

 For Alice, Alison, and Alyx

PUFFIN BOOKS
Published by the Penguin Group
Penguin Young Readers Group, 345 Hudson Street, New York, New York 10014, U.S.A.
Penguin Group (Canada), 90 Eglinton Avenue East, Suite 700, Toronto, Ontario, Canada M4P 2Y3 (a division of Pearson Penguin Canada Inc.)
Penguin Books Ltd, 80 Strand, London WC2R 0RL, England
Penguin Ireland, 25 St Stephen's Green, Dublin 2, Ireland (a division of Penguin Books Ltd)
Penguin Group (Australia), 250 Camberwell Road, Camberwell, Victoria 3124, Australia (a division of Pearson Australia Group Pty Ltd)
Penguin Books India Pvt Ltd, 11 Community Centre, Panchsheel Park, New Delhi - 110 017, India
Penguin Group (NZ), 67 Apollo Drive, Rosedale, North Shore 0632, New Zealand (a division of Pearson New Zealand Ltd)
Penguin Books (South Africa) (Pty) Ltd, 24 Sturdee Avenue, Rosebank, Johannesburg 2196, South Africa

Registered Offices: Penguin Books Ltd, 80 Strand, London WC2R 0RL, England

Published in Great Britain by Macmillan Children's Books, 2005
First published in the United States by Dial Books for Young Readers, a division of Penguin Young Readers Group, 2006
Published by Puffin Books, a division of Penguin Young Readers Group, 2008

7 9 10 8 6

Text copyright © Julia Donaldson, 2005
Illustrations copyright © Axel Scheffler, 2005
All rights reserved

THE LIBRARY OF CONGRESS HAS CATALOGED THE DIAL BOOKS FOR YOUNG READERS EDITION AS FOLLOWS:
Donaldson, Julia.
Charlie Cook's favorite book / Julia Donaldson ; illustrated by Axel Scheffler
p. cm.
Summary: A circular tale in which each new book character is reading about the next, beginning and ending with Charlie Cook.
ISBN: 978-0-8037-3142-4 (hc)
[1. Books and reading—Fiction. 2. Stories in rhyme.] I. Scheffler, Axel, ill. II. Title.
PZ8.3.D7235Cha 2006 [E]—dc22 2005021749

Puffin Books ISBN 978-0-14-241138-4
Printed in the United States of America
Except in the United States of America, this book is sold subject to the condition that
it shall not, by way of trade or otherwise, be lent, re-sold, hired out, or otherwise
circulated without the publisher's prior consent in any form of binding or cover
other than that in which it is published and without a similar condition
including this condition being imposed on the subsequent purchaser.

The publisher does not have any control over and does not assume
any responsibility for author or third-party Web sites or their content.

Charlie Cook's Favorite Book

Julia Donaldson

illustrated by Axel Scheffler

PUFFIN BOOKS

Once upon a time there was a boy
  called Charlie Cook
Who curled up in a cozy chair
  and read his favorite book . . .

About a leaky pirate ship
that very nearly sank
And a pirate chief who got the blame
and had to walk the plank.
The chief swam to an island
and went digging with his hook.

At last he found a treasure chest,
and in it was a book . . .

About a girl called Goldilocks,
and three indignant bears
Who cried, "Who's had our porridge?
Who's been sitting on our chairs?"

They went into the bedroom,
and Baby Bear said, "Look!
She's in my bed, and what is more,
she's got my favorite book . . ."

AS HE READ ALOUD A JOKE HE'D FOUND
(INSIDE HIS FAVORITE BOOK) . . .

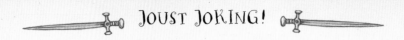

About Rowena Reddalot,
a very well-read frog,

Who jumped upon a lily pad

and jumped upon a log,

Then jumped into the library
that stood beside the brook,

 And went "Reddit! Reddit! Reddit!"
as she jumped upon a book . . .

About an oak tree full of birds.
Each bird had built a nest,
And they had a competition
to decide which one was best.

They chose an owl to judge it,
and the winner was a rook
Whose nest was lined with pages
from his very favorite book . . .

About a girl who saw

a flying saucer in the sky.

Some small green men were in it

and they waved as they flew by.

She tugged her mother's sleeve and said,

"Look, Mum, what I've just seen!"

But Mum said, "Hush, I'm trying to read

my favorite magazine . . ."

About a wicked jewel thief
who stole the king's best crown

ADVERTISEMENT

Doctor Foster's

Patented Galoshes!

NEW!

"I never go to Gloucester
without them!"
says a delighted Doctor Foster.

But then got stuck behind some sheep, which slowed his car right down.

The king got on the phone and soon the cops had caught the crook,

SITUATIONS
VACANT

GOVERNESS required for Lady Mary, aged 7. The child is sadly quite contrary. She insists she sees aliens in the garden. A strict governess is required, who can curb this vivid imagination.

Apply with references to Lady Fotherington, The Old Rookery, Banbury Cross.

And flung him into prison, where he read his favorite book…

PRISON LIBRARY
DO NOT DAMAGE

Åbout a greedy crocodile

who got fed up with fish

And went on land to try to find

some other kind of dish.

He went into a bookshop
and he there grew even greedier

While reading (on page 90
of a large encyclopedia) . . .

CAKE: a mixture of nice things, usually baked in the oven. It is eaten for dessert and on special occasions like birthdays and Christmas.

THE QUEEN'S BIRTHDAY CAKE

It took six trucks to carry the Cocoa Munchies for the queen's birthday cake to the palace. The cake also required 4,276 chocolate bars and 739 bags of marshmallows. The special extra-large cake tin was made by the Royal Blacksmith, using 2,647 melted-down horseshoes.

FAMOUS CAKE-EATERS

The world's most famous cake-eaters are the Bunn twins of York, England. At the age of six they became the youngest ever winners of the York Festival Cake-Eating Competition. At ten, they had to be taken to the hospital after knocking each other out while both reaching for the same slice of cake. (Their dog then ate the cake.)

About the biggest birthday cake the world had ever seen. A team of royal cakemakers had made it for the queen.

The cake was so delicious
that a famous spaceman took
A slice of it to Jupiter.
He also took a book . . .

About a ghost who glided
round a castle every night.

Carrying her head and
giving everyone a fright.

She kept it up till morning,
then she found a shady nook

And put her head back on again
to read her favorite book . . .

About a cozy armchair,
and a boy called Charlie Cook.

SHIVER ME TIMBERS

FAIRY TALES
FROM A FORGOTTEN ISLAND

THE BEARO ANNUAL

JOUST JOKING!

STORIES of
REAL BIRDS